Immortals

HERO

Warrior Princess

Steve Barlow and Steve Skidmore
Illustrated by Jack Lawrence

Franklin Watts
First published in Great Britain in 2016 by The Watts Publishing Group

PB ISBN 978 1 4451 5101 4
ebook ISBN 978 1 4451 5117 5
Library ebook ISBN 978 1 4451 5118 2

1 3 5 7 9 10 8 6 4 2

Printed and bound by CPI Group (UK) Ltd, Croydon, CR0 4YY

Franklin Watts

How to be a hero

This book is not like others you have read. This is a choose-your-own-destiny book where YOU are the hero of the adventure.

Each section of this book is numbered. At the end of most sections, you will have to make a choice. Each choice will take you to a different section of the book.

If you choose correctly, you will succeed. But be careful. If you make a bad choice, you may have to start the adventure again. If this happens, make sure you learn from your mistake!

Go to the next page to start your adventure. And remember, don't be a zero, be a hero!

You are a warrior princess. You rule over the Kingdom of the North, a land of ice and snow.

You use your fighting skills to protect your people, and you have a magical ability. You can communicate with the beasts of the frozen wastes. Polar bears, reindeer and snow leopards are among the many animals that help you to protect your kingdom from enemies who wish to destroy it.

Your land is kept frozen by the magical Ice Diamonds. These are held in the Crystal Caverns, protected by highly trained warriors called the Guardians. By keeping these valuable diamonds safe, you ensure that your people's way of life can continue in harmony with the animals of the kingdom.

Go to 1.

1

You are practising your archery skills with your new bow in the courtyard of your ice palace. You have only shot three arrows when Whitewing, your frost owl, flies down and settles on your arm.

"What is it, Whitewing?" you ask.

The frost owl replies, "The Ice Mother wishes to speak to you immediately."

The Ice Mother is the wise woman who gives you advice and guidance in ruling your kingdom.

To go to the Ice Mother straight away, go to 19.

To finish your archery practice first, go to 49.

2

"We cannot surrender the diamonds," you say. "We will fight and destroy the enemy!"

"As you wish," says Freya.

Soon you have gathered the remaining Guardians together. You order the gates to be opened and charge out.

The ground beneath you shakes as the enemy opens fire. A fireball explodes in front of you, throwing you from the back of your wolf.

You look up and see the raised leg of the ice walker above you, ready to crush you.

Go to 28.

3

You draw your sword from its sheath. You swing the blade and kill several of the creatures, but there are too many of them. Their deadly teeth snap at your body. There is only one thing to do!

Go to 28.

4

You ride towards the enemy, shooting arrows as swiftly as you can. However, the arrows just bounce off the Outlanders' armour, so you unsheathe your sword and guide your snow wolf between the rivers of flame that are flashing around you.

You head towards the leading rider and leap onto the back of his icetrack.

Go to 39.

5

"Who are these Outlanders?" you ask the Ice Mother.

"They are fighters from the Southlands, led by Professor Mekanik. He is a man driven by greed and hatred. He wishes to take our Ice Diamonds and sell them to the highest bidder. If he succeeds then our climate will change, the ice will melt and the kingdom will return to rock and water."

"We cannot allow this to happen," you say. "I have to stop them."

If you have already tried to restore the link to Freya, go to 30.

If not, go to 16.

6

You pick up the fire lance from where it fell. This could be useful later, you think.

Go to 44.

7

"We cannot delay," you say, urging the snow wolves forward. Slowly, they pull the sleigh onto the ice bridge. The ice creaks and groans under the weight.

"Princess! Look out!" the wolf pack leader cries.

Suddenly there is a loud crack and the ice bridge shatters. You are thrown from the sleigh and plummet downwards into the icy void. The wolves howl as they fall.

Go to 28.

8

You are soon heading towards the Crystal Caverns on the back of Ragnor. The glacial eagle's wings cut through the air as you speed above the great ice plains.

Ahead of you are black storm clouds. As you fly into the storm, bolts of lightning flash. Snow and ice tear at your body.

"I cannot see a way ahead," Ragnor says as you urge him on through the storm.

To try to find shelter, go to 38.

To return to your palace, go to 28.

9

You are met by Freya. She bows. "Welcome, Princess. Thank you for coming. The Outlanders got into the Crystal Caverns, but we fought them off. We have taken losses but the Ice Diamonds are safe, at least for now."

Freya leads you to the central cavern. In the middle is a huge ice sculpture of a snowflake. The Ice Diamonds are resting on each of the snowflake's six sides.

At that moment another Guardian rushes in. "The Outlanders want to talk. If we do not talk, their leader says they will destroy the Caverns."

To fight the Outlanders immediately, go to 47.

To talk to the Outlanders, go to 36.

10

You know that time is running out, so you command the wolves on through the raging storm.

Eventually the sky clears and you find yourself at the foot of the Frosty Mountains, which stand between you and the Crystal Caverns. These mountains are home to vampire ice bats whose deadly bite freezes their victim's blood.

"Should we go through the mountains? Or take the longer, safer way around them?" the wolf pack leader asks.

To go through the mountains, go to 40.
To go around the mountains, go to 46.

11

"How will I get to the Caverns in time to help the Guardians?" you ask.

"There are two choices," says the Ice Mother. "You can fly on the back of Ragnor, the great glacial eagle or ride on a sleigh pulled by snow wolves. Flying would normally get you there faster, but ice storms are moving in from the east. If they strike, then even Ragnor will not be able to fly through them. It will be slower, but I think you should take the sleigh."

If you wish to fly to the Caverns, go to 33.

If you wish to travel with the snow wolves, go to 24.

12

You urge your snow wolves on towards the entrance. Behind you the icetracks belch out blazing jets of fire that crackle around you.

The entrance is getting nearer when suddenly another icetrack rider scoots out in front of you, blocking the way into the Caverns. The rider was waiting for you! A sheet of flame spirals your way, but you just manage to avoid it.

To attack the rider with your sword, go to 39.

To call to the Caverns for help, go to 25.

13

You head into the cave to take shelter.

You light a snow lantern, but as you do, the air is filled with gigantic flying creatures. Your heart misses a beat; they are vampire ice bats! Their venomous bite turns blood to ice!

"Stop your attack!" you command, but you have no control over these fearsome creatures. You try to get out of the cave, but the huge swarm is blocking the way.

If you want to fight the ice bats, go to 3.

If you would rather use the moonstone pendant, go to 28.

14

You leap from the wolf, shooting arrows from your bow. You hit several bats, but they continue to close in on you.

"Stop your attack!" you command, but you have no control over these evil creatures.

To try to escape from the bats, go to 32.

To use your sword, go to 37.

15

You race across the frozen lake as Professor Mekanik sends fireball after fireball at you. You veer away trying to avoid the deadly missiles, but the fireballs melt the frozen lake all around you, sending you crashing into the icy water.

Go to 28.

16

"Can you restore the link to the Crystal Caverns?" you ask the Ice Mother.

She shakes her head. "The ice mirror in the Crystal Caverns must have been damaged. Until it can be fixed there is no way to speak to the Guardians."

If you have found out more about the Outlanders, go to 30.

If not, go to 5.

17

You head towards the front entrance of the Caverns. But as you approach there is a loud crack and the air is filled with shards of ice. A wall of ice near to the Caverns shatters and a hidden troop of Outlander icetrack riders crashes through. Smoky fire belches from their flamethrowers.

You have been ambushed!

To fight the enemy, go to 4.

To try to get to the entrance of the Caverns, go to 12.

18

You dismount from the snow wolf and carefully make your way towards the rider.

When you are within striking distance, you give a signal to the wolves. They charge forward and the icetrack rider spins around to fight off the attack.

Taking advantage of the diversion you somersault onto the back of the machine.

To use your sword, go to 39.

To knock the rider from the machine, go to 27.

19

You make your way to the Ice Mother's chamber. "You sent for me," you say.

She nods. "Our kingdom is in grave danger." She beckons you over to a large mirror made of ice. The Ice Mother uses this magical mirror to see what is happening across the kingdom.

"I have received a message for help from the Crystal Caverns." The Ice Mother waves her hand in front of the ice mirror and the image of a female warrior appears.

You recognise Freya, the captain of the Guardians of the Ice Diamonds. Her face is grim. "Princess, thank goodness you are there! We are under attack! We need your help now!"

To head for the Crystal Caverns immediately, go to 26.

To find out more from Freya, go to 35.

20

"We cannot surrender the diamonds," you say. "But the enemy is too strong for us to fight. I will take the diamonds to a place of safety."

"Then we will stay here and cover your escape," says Freya.

"But that will mean certain death," you say.

"We are prepared for that," she replies.

If you wish to leave the Guardians, go to 34.

If you don't, go to 29.

21

"Come, we'll leave the sleigh behind," you say to the wolves. You release them from their harness, and lead them over the fragile bridge. You reach the other side.

"Princess, climb on my back," the pack leader says. You climb on carefully and continue on your way into the heart of the mountains. You wonder if you'll be fast enough without the sleigh.

Suddenly the air is filled with screeching, and you look up to see a swarm of vampire ice bats. They are heading towards you with their deadly teeth bared.

To use your bow against these creatures, go to 14.

To use your sword, go to 37.

22

You soon pass through the mountains and find yourself looking down on the Crystal Caverns, which lie on the shores of a huge frozen lake.

You are surprised to find that there is no sign of the Outlanders. You wonder if you are too late... You make your way down towards the Caverns through a narrow ravine.

"Look!" the wolf leader says.

Suddenly you stop dead. Ahead of you is a figure sitting astride a vehicle. It's a mechanical icetrack used by the Outlanders. The rider has his back to you, but is blocking your way.

If you wish to shoot an arrow at the Outlander, go to 41.

If you want to avoid bloodshed, go to 18.

23

You collect the diamonds and head towards the entrance with your snow wolves. Freya opens the gate and you leave the Caverns.

Professor Mekanik's voice rings out. "You have made the right decision."

I know, you think.

At that moment the sky starts to grow dark. You look up and see hundreds of birds flying towards you. Eagles, ospreys and skuas dive in to attack the Outlanders. A deafening noise rises from the mountains. Polar bears, wolves, elk and hundreds of other animals charge forward. The beasts of the kingdom have answered your call! They attack the icetrack riders.

You quickly race your wolf across the frozen lake, away from the Caverns. Professor Mekanik fights off an eagle and speeds after you in his ice walker.

If you picked up the icetrack rider's fire lance, go to 42.

If you didn't, go to 15.

24

"I must get to the Crystal Caverns safely, so I will travel with the snow wolves. They may also help me to fight against the Outlanders."

"This is your choice," says the Ice Mother. "I hope you have made the right decision."

Go to 48.

25

You guide your wolf past the deadly fireballs that explode around you.

"Open the gates!" you scream. "Open the gates!"

Ahead of you the great ice gates slowly open and you urge the wolves on.

The icetracks speed after you, but you are too quick. You hurtle through the Cavern's entrance as the gates crash shut behind you. You have made it!

Go to 9.

26

"There is no time to lose," you cry. "I will go to the Crystal Caverns immediately!"

The Ice Mother shakes her head. "Be patient, my child," she says. "We need to know more."

You realise that she is right. You turn back to the mirror.

Go to 35.

27

Before the rider can strike with his fire lance, you crash into him and push him off. As he tumbles to the ground, the hot blade of his lance cuts through the track of his machine and it topples over. The fire lance falls into the snow. You leap to the ground as the icetrack crashes on top of your enemy, trapping him underneath.

If you wish to take the Outlander's fire lance, go to 6.

If you don't want to, go to 44.

28

You grasp hold of the moonstone pendant. "Ice and snow, home I go," you say.

A whirlwind of snowflakes engulfs you as you pass through time and space. You find yourself back in your ice palace. The Ice Mother stands before you.

"You made the wrong choice," she says sadly. "You must begin your task again."

If you wish to fly to the Caverns on the glacial eagle, go to 33.

If you wish to travel with the snow wolves, go to 24.

29

"I will not leave you," you say. "I have a plan."

You lean from the gallery and cry out. "Beasts from the Kingdom of the North, your Princess needs your help!" The sound of your voice carries across the lake and into the skies.

You hear your plea echoing around the distant mountains.

Professor Mekanik laughs. "There is no one or anything to help you, poor Princess. Surrender or die!"

"We must surrender then," you say.

"No!" cries Freya.

"Do not worry," you tell her. "Trust me."

Go to 23.

30

"You must head to the Crystal Caverns immediately," says the Ice Mother. "But you will need this."

She places a silver cord around your

neck. On it hangs a snowflake-shaped pendant. "This magical jewel is made from moonstone," she tells you. "If you find yourself in danger and cannot escape, then call on its power. It will bring you back to this time and place where you can restart your quest."

You must now decide how you will get to the Crystal Caverns.

If you wish to ask for the Ice Mother's advice, go to 11.

To decide for yourself, go to 43.

31

You make your way around the frozen lake to the rear entrance to the Caverns. You stop outside the concealed gate.

"Freya! Open the gate!" you command. If the Guardians still control the Caverns, they will know your voice and let you in.

After a few seconds an ice door slowly opens and you lead the wolves inside the Caverns.

Go to 9.

32

You leap back onto the wolf pack leader. "Run with all your heart!" you command.

"Yes, my Princess," the wolf says.

The snow wolves obey and race along the mountain track at incredible speed. The bats continue to give chase, but they cannot catch you. You are safe! You slow down and continue your journey through the mountains.

Go to 22.

33

"I must get to the Caverns quickly," you say. "I will fly with Ragnor."

"I hope that you have made the right choice," says the Ice Mother.

Go to 8.

34

"The kingdom will remember your bravery," you say.

You head to the central cavern, pick up the diamonds and head towards the back entrance of the cave with the snow wolves. You say goodbye to Freya and open the gate.

Suddenly a volley of fireballs explodes around you. The Outlanders have found the rear entrance! They continue to blast at the cavern walls. Tons of snow and ice crash down, blocking your way back into the cavern. You are trapped!

Go to 28.

35

"Who is attacking you, Freya?" you ask.

"Outlanders from the South!" she replies. "They want the Ice Diamonds. They are armed and riding mechanical icetracks equipped with flamethrowers! We are holding them off, but we have taken losses. We need your—" but before Freya can finish, the ice mirror turns black.

The Ice Mother looks grim. "The connection is broken. The Outlanders must have got into the Crystal Caverns."

If you wish to discover more about the Outlanders, go to 5.

To try to restore the link to Freya, go to 16.

36

"We will talk to them," you decide.

You make your way to a gallery high in the Caverns, where you can view the attackers.

Outside the Caverns stands a troop of icetrack riders, grouped behind a huge mechanical ice walker, which is shaped like a massive, metal spider crab.

Standing on top of the ice walker is a strange-looking figure. He sees you and speaks through the machine's loudspeakers.

"I am Professor Mekanik! Give me the Ice Diamonds and I will let you go. If you refuse, my followers will take them by force. You have fifteen minutes to decide!"

If you decide to fight the enemy, go to 2.

If you wish to try to take the diamonds to a safe place, go to 20.

37

You take out your sword as the swarm hits.

You swing your blade and kill several of the deadly creatures before they can plunge their teeth into your body.

But you are fighting a losing battle; there are too many of the creatures for you to deal with.

You cry out in pain as one of the bats plunges its teeth into your neck. The venom begins to spread through your body, freezing your blood.

You only have one way out of this situation!

Go to 28.

38

You guide Ragnor down in search of shelter.

"Land on that ridge," you say pointing ahead. The eagle descends onto a rocky outcrop and you dismount. To your left there is a cave in the rock wall.

To head into the cave, go to 13.

To remain on the outcrop, go to 45.

If you want to return to your ice palace, go to 28.

39

You thrust at the rider with your sword, but he parries your blow with a fire lance. It slices through your blade, leaving you helpless.

He swings the fire lance at your head.

Go to 28.

40

You steer the wolves towards the mountains and up a narrow path of ice. The way is dangerous, but you know you have to get to the Crystal Caverns as quickly as you can.

As you get higher into the mountains, the path gets narrower and you arrive at an ice bridge that crosses a deep ravine.

"I'm not sure we can get across this bridge with the sleigh. It may be too heavy," the wolf pack leader says.

If you decide to abandon the sleigh and walk across, go to 21.

If you wish to continue in the sleigh, go to 7.

41

You carefully nock an arrow to your bowstring and shoot it at the rider. It hits him, but bounces off his metal armour.

The rider spins around and laughs. “Professor Mekanik knew help would come this way! We are ready for you!” A great sheet of flame spews from the icetrack’s flamethrower towards you.

There is no time to avoid it!

Go to 28.

42

You lead the ice walker across the lake, keeping too far ahead for it to use its weapons. Its engine spews clouds of smoke into the air as its cogs speed up. Then suddenly you steer your wolf around and head for the ice walker. Professor Mekanik shoots oily fire from the machine’s flamethrower, but you avoid the blast.

You take hold of the fire lance, turn it on and speed through the legs of the ice walker. You thrust the lance upwards, piercing the metal belly and the machine's boiler. Hot coal and ash crash out onto the frozen lake.

The walker crunches to a halt, its engine gears grinding, as the ice underneath it begins to melt. You speed away before turning to see the heavy machine plunging into the dark, cold depths of the lake.

You head back towards the Caverns to find that the icetrack riders have sped away, pursued by the beasts of your kingdom.

Go to 50.

43

You know that you have two choices. You can fly on the back of Ragnor, the great glacial eagle or ride on a sleigh pulled by snow wolves. The quickest way is to fly, the safest way is to travel on the sleigh.

If you wish to fly to the Caverns, go to 33.

If you wish to travel with the snow wolves, go to 24.

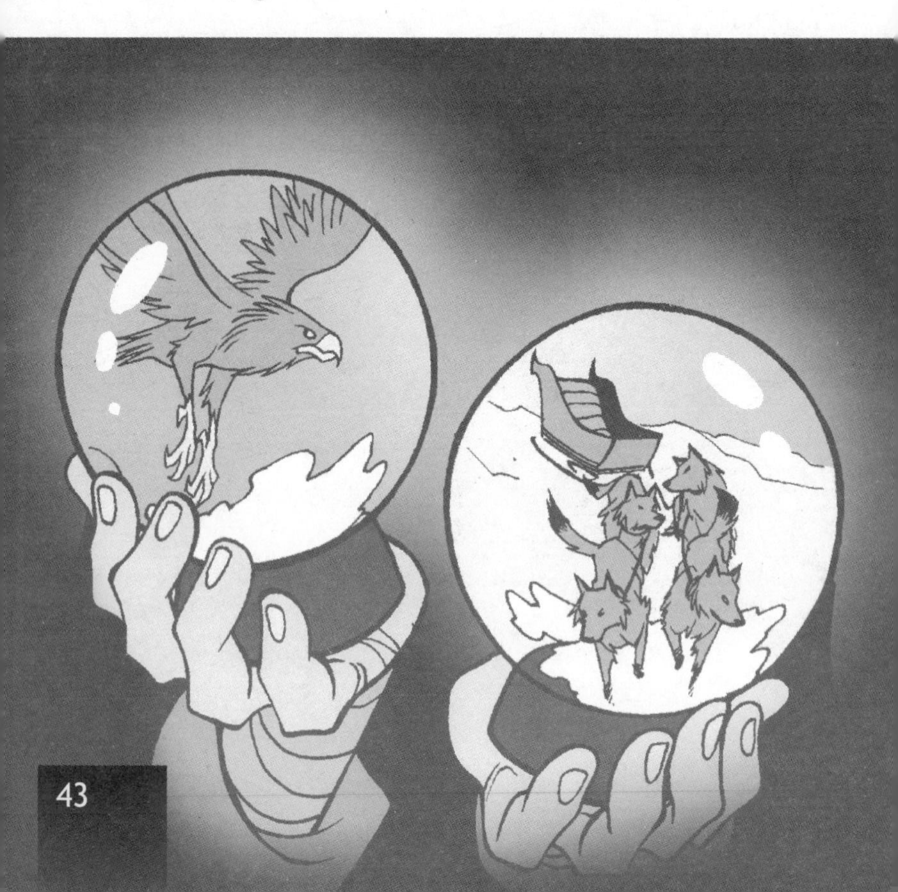

44

Leaving your defeated enemy, you climb onto the back of a wolf and race towards the Crystal Caverns, hoping that you are in time to save the Ice Diamonds.

To head to the front entrance, go to 17.
To head to the back entrance, go to 31.

45

You nestle under Ragnor's wing, waiting for the storm to die down.

Sometime later, the sky suddenly turns to blue and the sun beats down hot and bright. The air around you becomes warm. The snow and ice around you begin to melt at incredible speed!

You realise that the Ice Diamonds must have been taken from the Crystal Caverns and your land is changing forever. You have failed in your mission!

Go to 28.

46

You continue your journey around the mountains. After many hours of travelling, the snow and ice suddenly begin to melt. The wolves can no longer pull the sleigh through the slush. Your kingdom is melting away! You realise the Ice Diamonds have been taken. You have failed!

Go to 28.

47

"We must attack immediately," you say.

Freya shakes her head. "We are outnumbered, Princess. We cannot hope to beat the enemy in a fight. We must find another way to save the Ice Diamonds."

You realise that she is right.

Go to 36.

48

You are soon speeding to the Crystal Caverns. Four huge, white snow wolves pull your sleigh across the great ice plain.

"Princess, a storm is coming," you hear one of the wolves say. In the distance you see black storm clouds gathering. You know that time is short, so you urge the wolves on. "We must reach the Caverns!" you say. Bolts of lightning crash around and snow and ice shower down on you and the wolves.

To your left you can just make out a cave in a rock wall. This would be a perfect place to shelter from the storm.

To get out of the sleigh and lead the wolves into the cave, go to 13.

To carry on, go to 10.

49

"But I need to finish my archery practice, first, Whitewing. Just a few more arrows," you say.

The frost owl hoots noisily. "It is a matter of great importance. You must go immediately."

You know Whitewing is right.

Go to 19.

50

Sometime later, you are back in the Crystal Caverns having returned the Ice Diamonds to their rightful place.

Freya and the Guardians stand with you in front of the ice mirror. The communication with the Ice Mother has been restored and you tell her how you defeated Professor Mekanik.

She smiles. "You have done well, Princess. The kingdom is safe. You are a true hero!"

I HERO Quiz

Test yourself with this special quiz. It has been designed to see how much you remember about the book you've just read. Can you get all five answers right?

To download the answer sheets simply visit:

www.hachettechildrens.co.uk

Enter the "Teacher Zone" and search "Immortals".

Question 1

What type of animal is Ragnor?

A a snow wolf

B a glacial eagle

C a frost owl

D a snow leopard

Question 2

What does Professor Mekanik want?

A the Warrior Princess

B to become king

C the Ice Diamonds

D the Crystal Caverns

Question 3

Which animal attacks Professor Mekanik?

A a wolf

B a polar bear

C a reindeer

D an eagle

Question 4

Which weapon do you use to defeat the ice walker?

A a bow

B a sword

C a fire lance

D a flame thrower

Question 5

Who do you see first in the magic ice mirror?

A Freya

B Ice Mother

C Professor Mekanik

D Ragnor

About the 2Steves

"The 2Steves" are Britain's most popular writing double act for young people, specialising in comedy and adventure. They perform regularly in schools and libraries, and at festivals, taking the power of words and story to audiences of all ages.

Together they have written many books, including the *Crime Team* series. Find out what they've been up to at: **www.the2steves.net**

About the illustrator: Jack Lawrence

Jack Lawrence is a successful freelance comics illustrator, working on titles such as *A.T.O.M.*, Cartoon Network, *Doctor Who Adventures*, *2000 AD*, *Transformers* and *Spider-Man Tower of Power*. He also works as a freelance toy designer.

Jack lives in Maidstone in Kent with his partner and two cats.

Have you completed the I HERO Quests?

Battle with aliens in Tyranno Quest:

978 1 4451 0875 9 pb
978 1 4451 1345 6 ebook

978 1 4451 0876 6 pb
978 1 4451 1346 3 ebook

978 1 4451 0877 3 pb
978 1 4451 1347 0 ebook

978 1 4451 0878 0 pb
978 1 4451 1348 7 ebook

Defeat the Red Queen in Blood Crown Quest:

978 1 4451 1499 6 pb
978 1 4451 1503 0 ebook

978 1 4451 1500 9 pb
978 1 4451 1504 7 ebook

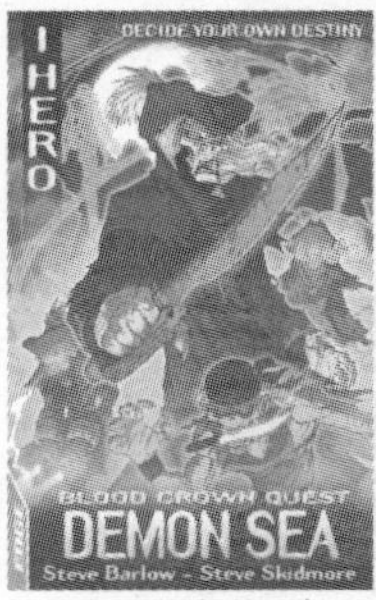

978 1 4451 1501 6 pb
978 1 4451 1505 4 ebook

978 1 4451 1502 3 pb
978 1 4451 1506 1 ebook

Save planet Earth in Atlantis Quest:

978 1 4451 2867 2 pb
978 1 4451 2868 9 ebook

978 1 4451 2870 2 pb
978 1 4451 2871 9 ebook

978 1 4451 2876 4 pb
978 1 4451 2877 1 ebook

978 1 4451 2873 3 pb
978 1 4451 2874 0 ebook

More I HERO Immortals

978 1 4451 4081 0 pb
978 1 4451 4082 7 eBook

You are the last Dragon Warrior. A dark, evil force stirs within the Iron Mines. Grull the Cruel's army is on the march! YOU must stop Grull.

978 1 4451 4088 9 pb
978 1 4451 4087 2 eBook

You are a noble mermaid – your father is King Edmar. The Tritons are attacking your home of Coral City. YOU must save the Merrow people by finding the Lady of the Sea.

978 1 4451 4084 1 pb
978 1 4451 4085 8 eBook

You are Olympian, a superhero. Your enemy, Doctor Robotic, is turning people into mind slaves. Now YOU must put a stop to his plans before it's too late!

978 1 4451 3958 6 pb
978 1 4451 3961 6 eBook

You are a young wizard. The evil Witch Queen has captured Prince Bron. Now YOU must rescue him before she takes control of Nine Mountain kingdom!